First published in Great Britain 2024 by Farshore
An imprint of HarperCollins*Publishers*
1 London Bridge Street, London SE1 9GF
www.farshore.co.uk

HarperCollins*Publishers*
Macken House, 39/40 Mayor Street Upper,
Dublin 1, Ireland D01 C9W8

ISBN 978 0 00 867058 0
Printed in the United Kingdom
1

A CIP catalogue record for this book is available from the British Library.

Stay safe online. Farshore is not responsible for content hosted by third parties.

All statistics and facts correct as of March 2024.

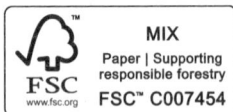

	MIX
FSC www.fsc.org	Paper | Supporting responsible forestry FSC™ C007454

This book contains FSC™ certified paper and other controlled
sources to ensure responsible forest management.

For more information visit: www.harpercollins.co.uk/green

Topps

MATCH ATTAX

TRADING CARD GAME

EXTRA TIME

TEASERS

OVER 70 FOOTY PUZZLES

WELCOME TO
MATCH ATTAX
EXTRA TIME TEASERS!

★ ★ ★

This **EPIC** book is bursting with **FOOTY FACTS** and **SUPER STATS** that will help you master the exciting world of **FOOTBALL**!

Discover the secrets behind every position on the pitch and what gives the game's superstars the edge over their opponents – then take on our **TOP TRIVIA QUIZZES** and **PRO PUZZLES** to see if you've got what it takes to lift the trophy!

Get ready ...
It's time for kick off!

MATCH ATTAX MIX-UP

**A Match Attax card has been divided into five strips.
Your task is to put the card back together. Can you
work out what order the strips need to go in?**

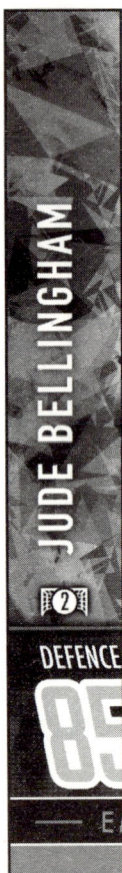

CORRECT ORDER:

2 4 3 5 1

6

BROKEN RECORDS

These football records sound incredible, but some aren't true. Write true or false next to each one!

1 Manchester United have won the English top-flight league title 20 times. More than any other club. — **T**

2 The all-time top scorer in the German top-flight league is Jadon Sancho for Borussia Dortmund. — **F**

3 The most goals scored by one player in a single Spanish top-flight season is 50, by Lionel Messi in just 37 matches. — **T**

4 The fastest ever French top-flight league hat-trick was scored in four minutes and 30 seconds, by Loïs Openda for Lens.

5 A standard regulation football pitch in top-flight leagues is 125 metres wide.

6 Norwich have been relegated from the English top-flight league six times – more than any other club.

7 No club has won the Scottish top-flight league more times than Rangers, with 103 titles to their name.

8 Vivianne Miedema has scored 203 goals in the English top-flight women's league, more than any other player.

9 Liverpool's Anfield is the smallest stadium ever to host an English top-flight league match.

10 Napoli won the 2022-23 Italian top-flight league title with an incredible 28 wins from 38 matches.

GOAL FRENZY

How many times can you see the word GOAL in the word grid
below? It could go forwards, backwards, up, down or diagonally!
Time yourself and count how many times you can find it!

G	D	A	O	S	B	L	M	G	A	L	B	G
B	O	G	A	O	E	A	B	G	I	D	R	O
M	L	A	D	I	M	O	U	O	O	S	M	A
O	D	U	L	A	O	G	A	A	E	A	G	L
O	A	R	M	G	R	D	B	L	M	B	L	A
G	O	A	L	U	G	L	A	I	D	L	U	S
S	B	G	E	B	E	G	S	G	R	O	A	A
L	D	U	I	L	L	O	E	L	A	O	G	B
A	M	G	R	O	D	A	M	A	B	A	D	M
O	B	O	A	M	B	L	O	O	L	G	D	O
G	A	A	U	S	A	G	E	G	E	A	E	B
B	S	L	E	D	E	I	M	D	O	I	O	S
G	O	G	O	A	L	B	L	R	A	U	B	G

I found _____GOALS in

_____minutes,_____seconds!

8

DIFFICULTY:

TOP-SECRET TACTICS

The game is coming to an end and your team needs a goal. Your head coach has passed you a coded note with tactics on. Can you crack the code?

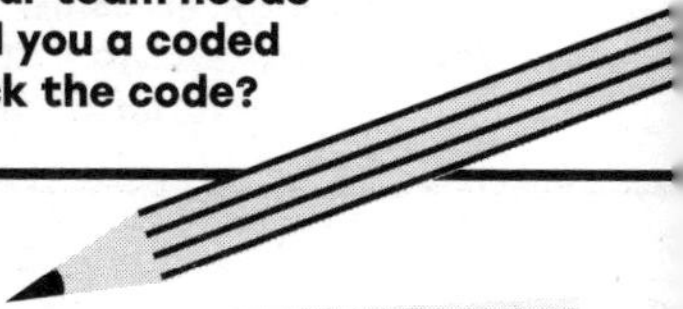

20 8 5 9 18 12 5 6 20 21 3 11
9 19 20 9 18 5 4.
1 20 20 1 3 11 20 8 5 13!

CODE BREAKING RULES

Each number represents where the letter comes in the alphabet. For example, 1 is A, 18 is R and 26 is Z.

THE CODED MESSAGE IS:

_ _ _ _ _ _ _ _ _ _ _

_ _ _ _ _ _ _ .

_ _ _ _ _ _ _ _ _ !

Answer on page 78.

9

VAR REPLAY

The ref needs confirmation on a key decision, as only two of these instant replay images match exactly. Can you work out which two are the same?

_____ and _____ are the same.

Answer on page 79.

KANE'S RECORDS

Harry Kane might play for Bayern Munich now, but he is a Tottenham legend. Draw a line between these epic statements and their answers!

Test yourself! Set a timer for 1 minute. Can you connect them all in time?

1 Harry is Tottenham's record English top-flight goal scorer, with how many goals?

0

2 Kane made his Tottenham first-team debut at this age.

10, 18, 37

3 What shirt numbers did Harry wear representing Tottenham?

4 Kane scored this many hat-tricks whilst wearing Tottenham colours.

18

5 Harry is a team player and laid on this many league assists for his Tottenham teammates.

213

8

6 How many red cards did Kane receive in his 12 years as a Tottenham player?

46

BENDING SHOT

It's the last minute and this star striker has a powerful effort from long range. Can you work out which shot ends up in the goal?

(A)

(B)

(C)

Test yourself! Set a timer for 30 seconds. Can you get to the goal in time?

Answer on page 79.

DIFFICULTY: ⚽ ⚽ ⚽

LEAGUE OF THEIR OWN

Below are teams from some of the best leagues in the world, but only one from each row has won their league title – do you know which?

SPAIN

REAL ZARAGOZA — BARCELONA — RCD ESPANYOL — VILLARREAL

FRANCE

LE HAVRE — LORIENT — CLERMONT FOOT — PARIS SAINT-GERMAIN

GERMANY

SC FREIBURG — UNION BERLIN — BAYERN MUNICH — VFL BOCHUM

ENGLAND

MANCHESTER CITY — WEST HAM — FULHAM — LUTON

ITALY

ATALANTA — EMPOLI — INTER MILAN — UDINESE

SCOTLAND

ST MIRREN — ROSS COUNTY — CELTIC — ST JOHNSTONE

SPAIN _____   ENGLAND _____

FRANCE _____   ITALY _____

GERMANY _____   SCOTLAND _____

PREMIER PITCH

How quickly can you find your way through this footy pitch maze?

START

FINISH

I did it in ____ minutes, ____ seconds!

SUPERSTAR NAMES

A manager has selected a forward line of five of the best players in the world. Read the clues and try to complete their names on the team sheet!

1. R _ _ H _ O _ D

This Red Devil knows how to hit the mark-us!

2. M _ _ D I _ O _

Good luck making this Spurs midfielder mad ...

3. H _ _ L _ _ D

Har you sure this City striker isn't the best in the world?

4. K _ D _ S

You've got to give kudos to Mohammed!

5. _ E S S _

This FIFA World Cup-winning legend is never untidy!

Answers on page 81.

DIFFICULTY:

GERMAN LEAGUE

It's time to test your knowledge on Germany's top-flight league. Don't worry if you don't know all the answers. What's German for 'let's go!'? Auf geht's!

1 In the 2012-13 season, Bayern Munich scored a record number of points. But how many was it?

A. 91   **C.** 65
B. 24   **D.** 27   - - - - - - - - - - - - - - -

2 Real Madrid sensation Jude Bellingham used to play for this German giant.

A. Union Berlin
B. Eintracht Frankfurt
C. Borussia Dortmund
D. Bayer Leverkusen

- -

3 Which team came third in the 2022-23 German top-flight football season?

A. Bayern Munich
B. RB Leipzig
C. Borussia Dortmund
D. Union Berlin

- -

4 In the 2020-21 season, how many league goals did Robert Lewandowski score?

A. 65   **C.** 17
B. 41   **D.** 25

- - - - - - - - - - - -

5 How many players have scored hat-tricks on their German top-flight league debuts?

A. 7   **C.** 0
B. 1   **D.** 3   - - - - - - - - - - - - - -

6 Which German top-flight team play its home matches at the Weserstadion?

A. FC Augsburg
B. Eintracht Frankfurt
C. FC Köln
D. Werder Bremen

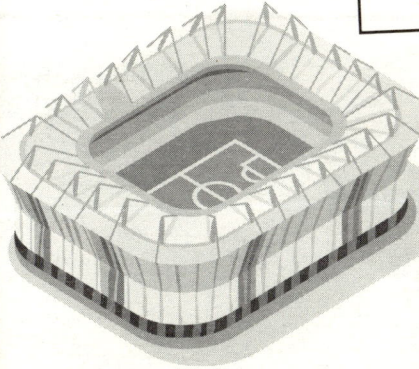

----

7 In which season did Bayern Munich and Borussia Dortmund both finish level on 71 points?

A. 2021-22
B. 2007-08
C. 2017-18
D. 2022-23

----

8 No one has won more German top-flight matches than this total legend.

A. Gregor Kobel
B. Thomas Müller
C. Manuel Neuer
D. Lukas Hradecky

----

9 Who is the highest scorer in German top-flight history?

A. Gerd Müller
B. Thomas Müller
C. Claudio Pizarro
D. Harry Kane

----

10 One of these team names doesn't actually exist in Germany's leagues. Which is it?

A. Hamburger SV
B. Cheeseburger XL
C. Dynamo Dresden
D. Mainz 05

Answers on page 81.

AROUND THE GROUNDS

**Every team plays at a stadium they call home.
Draw a line to match these top European
clubs with their correct grounds.**

CLUB	STADIUM

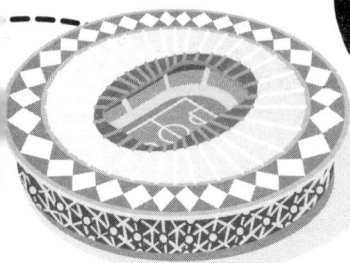

Test yourself! Set a timer for 30 seconds. Can you match them all in time?

CLUB	STADIUM
Borussia Dortmund	Old Trafford
Paris Saint-Germain	Parc des Princes
Manchester United	Stadio Diego Armando Maradona
SSC Napoli	BVB Stadion
Arsenal	Santiago Bernabéu Stadium
Real Madrid	Emirates Stadium

ATTACK OR DEFEND?

Each of these players is famous for thrilling fans around Europe, but what are they famous for – attacking or defending?

1. Álvaro Morata

----

2. Jude Bellingham

----

3. Marquinhos

----

4. Erling Haaland

----

5. Axel Witsel

----

6. João Félix

----

7. Bukayo Saka

----

8. Rúben Dias

Answers on page 81.

SQUAD NUMBERS

**Check out the shirt numbers below.
Do you know which legendary players wear
the number for each team as of 2024?**

1

LIVERPOOL:

11

ASTON VILLA:

20

WEST HAM:

8

MANCHESTER UNITED:

TOTTENHAM HOTSPUR:

MANCHESTER CITY:

ARSENAL:

CHELSEA:

Answers on page 81.

DIFFICULTY:

BALL CONTROL

The match is about to start but the practice balls need clearing off the pitch. How many are there?

There are _____ balls.

BETWEEN THE STICKS

The UEFA Women's Champions League has some of the best goalies in the world. Can you find them all in this word grid?

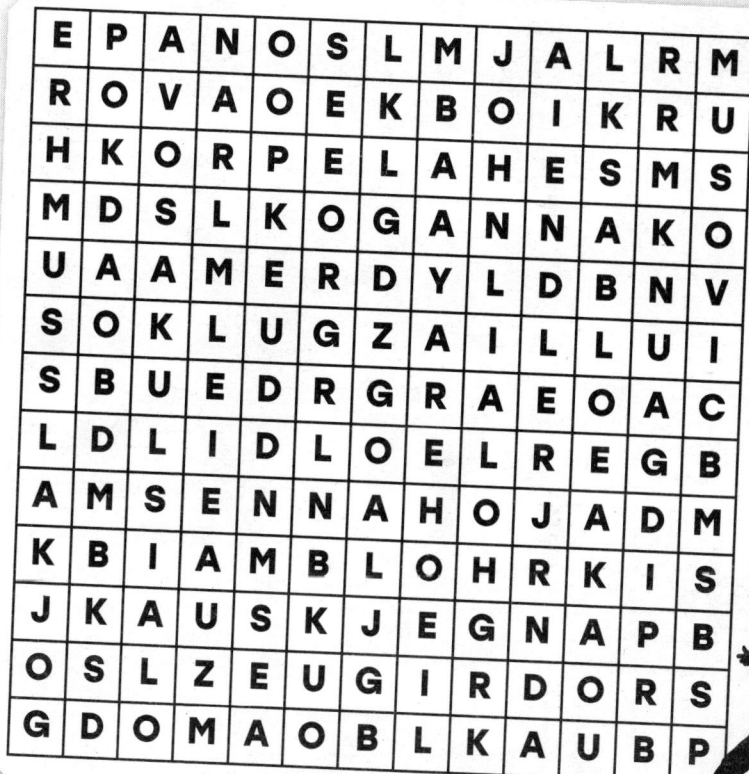

E	P	A	N	O	S	L	M	J	A	L	R	M
R	O	V	A	O	E	K	B	O	I	K	R	U
H	K	O	R	P	E	L	A	H	E	S	M	S
M	D	S	L	K	O	G	A	N	N	A	K	O
U	A	A	M	E	R	D	Y	L	D	B	N	V
S	O	K	L	U	G	Z	A	I	L	L	U	I
S	B	U	E	D	R	G	R	A	E	O	A	C
L	D	L	I	D	L	O	E	L	R	E	G	B
A	M	S	E	N	N	A	H	O	J	A	D	M
K	B	I	A	M	B	L	O	H	R	K	I	S
J	K	A	U	S	K	J	E	G	N	A	P	B
O	S	L	Z	E	U	G	I	R	D	O	R	S
G	D	O	M	A	O	B	L	K	A	U	B	P

○ Paños   ○ Mušović   ○ Endler

○ Kiedrzynek   ○ Lukášová   ○ Korpela

○ Rodríguez   ○ Johannes

I found them all in _____ minutes, _____ seconds.

DIFFICULTY:

ENGLISH LEAGUE

The best teams in England take each other on every week and we can't get enough. How well do you know the English top-flight league?

1 The most points scored by one club in a single season was 100. But who achieved it?

A. Manchester United
B. Arsenal
C. Luton
D. Manchester City

----

2 The fewest wins by one team in a single season was by Derby County in 2007-08. How many wins did they get?

A. 3   **C.** 1
B. 7   **D.** 2

----

3 The most matches played in a row was 310, by Brad Friedel. What position did he play?

A. Goalkeeper
B. Centre-back
C. Midfield
D. Forward

----

4 Which English top-flight player has scored the most direct free-kicks?

A. David Beckham
B. James Ward-Prowse
C. Miguel Almiron
D. Kyle Walker

----

5 Assist king Kevin De Bruyne was the quickest player to notch up 50 assists. How many matches did it take him?

A. 123   **C.** 1,001
B. 47   **D.** 23

6 How many goalkeepers have scored a goal in the English top-flight league?

A. 0   **C.** 6
B. 32   **D.** 14

----

7 Which team did Leicester hammer 9-0 to record the biggest away win in English top-flight history?

A. Burnley   **C.** Brighton
B. Bournemouth   **D.** Southampton

----

8 If you added up every result from every season of the English top-flight, which team would be in 1st place?

A. Chelsea   **C.** Liverpool
B. Manchester United   **D.** Wolves

9 Which of these English top-flight teams wears the famous colours of claret and blue?

A. Brighton
B. Aston Villa
C. Newcastle
D. Everton

10 Which English top-flight stadium has the highest capacity?

A. London Stadium
B. Old Trafford
C. Stamford Bridge
D. Emirates Stadium

Answers on page 82.

MYSTERY STARS

**These shady stars are keeping their identity in the
dark! Check out the clues for each player and have
a go at guessing who they really are.**

1
I play for Germany and
Barcelona, but I lifted the
trophy for Manchester City
in the 2022-23 season.

2
I'm a solid centre back.
I captain Liverpool and
inspire my teammates
across the pitch!

3
I play in the white of Real
Madrid. I scored 13 goals in
my first 14 matches after
joining the club!

4
I captain Barcelona.
I've been in the Barca
squad since making my
debut in 2010.

MATCH ATTAX MIX UP

Another Match Attax card has been divided into five strips. Your task is to put the card back together. Can you work out what order the strips need to go in?

1 **2** **3** **4** **5**

  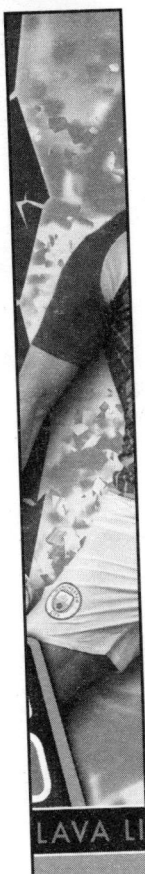  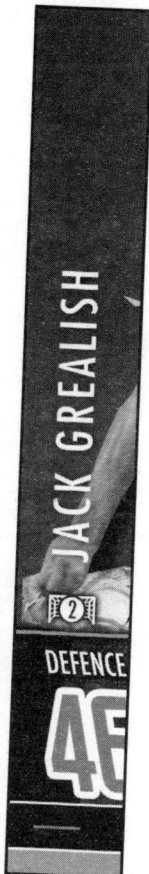

CORRECT ORDER:

____ ____ ____ ____ ____

Answer on page 83.

27

INTERNATIONAL GLORY

**Below are eight powerhouses of the international football world.
Can you fill in the missing letters to identify them?**

1. _ R _ _ I L

2. E _ _ L _ _ D

3. A R _ _ _ T _ _ A

4. _ _ A I _

5. M _ _ _ C _

6. U R _ G _ _ Y

7. _ _ P _ N

8. F _ _ N _ E

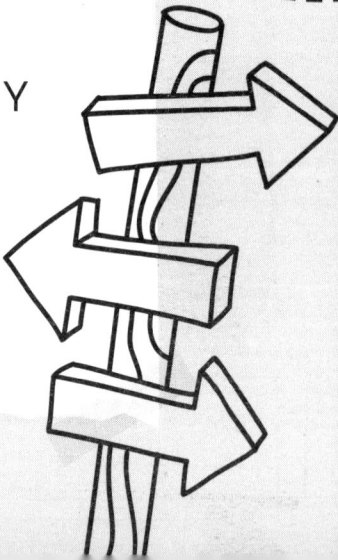

MYSTERY PLAYER 1

**Can you read the clues and identify which
mystery player is being described?**

I run the midfield of a title-challenging club in England.

I played for England at major tournaments in 2020 and 2022.

I was part of Chelsea's academy before breaking through at West Ham.

In 2023, I lifted the Europa Conference League trophy as captain.

THE MYSTERY PLAYER IS:

Answer on page 83.

TROPHY CABINETS

**Can you link the footy clubs below
to the trophies they won in 2023?**

Test yourself!
Set a timer for
1 minute. Can
you match
them all in
time?

West Ham

Scottish
Champions

Manchester City

German
Champions

Sevilla

Italian
Champions

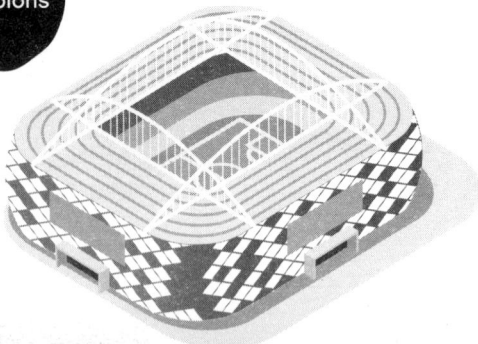

Barcelona

French
Champions

Paris Saint-Germain

Spanish Champions

Napoli

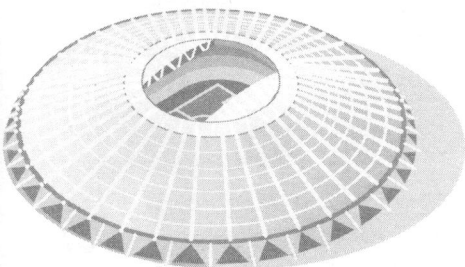

UEFA Champions League

Bayern Munich

UEFA Europa League

UEFA Europa Conference League

Celtic

Answers on page 84.

DIFFICULTY:

WOMEN'S LEAGUE

Exciting football played in front of packed stadiums – the women's English top-flight league has it all! How many of these questions can you answer?

1 How many clubs take part in a season of England's top-flight women's league?

A. 12   **C.** 23
B. 14   **D.** 8

----

2 Which team has won the current top tier the most?

A. Burnley
B. Southampton
C. Arsenal
D. Chelsea

----

3 Who was the league's top scorer during the 2022-23 season?

A. Khadija Shaw
B. Lauren James
C. Rachel Daly
D. Martha Thomas

----

4 Manchester United's highest league finish so far was ... ?

A. 8th   **C.** 14th
B. 2nd   **D.** 5th

A. Vivianne Miedema
B. Alessia Russo
C. Stina Blackstenius
D. Beth Mead

5 Which Arsenal striker is the league's all-time top scorer?

6 How many home matches in a row did Chelsea play without losing?

A. 14 **C.** 72
B. 38 **D.** 33

----

7 What is the highest attendance for a women's top-flight league match?

A. 60,160 **C.** 10,001
B. 102,398 **D.** 19,733

8 The youngest player to make their women's top-flight debut is Lauren James, but how old was she?

A. 21 **C.** 14
B. 16 **D.** 25

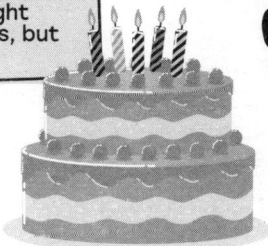

9 In 2020-21, which team only lost one match during the season?

A. Brighton
B. Aston Villa
C. Newcastle
D. Chelsea

----

10 What did Manchester City striker Jill Roord achieve just six days apart in 2020?

A. Scored two goals
B. Two hat-tricks
C. Two red cards
D. Four yellow cards

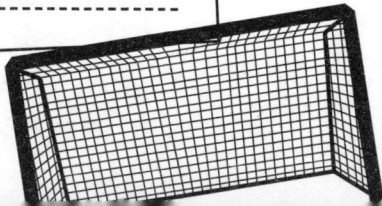

Answers on page 84.

MYSTERY PLAYER 2

Time for another player puzzle! Can you read the clues and identify who is being described?

I play for a top club that plays home matches in a sky blue shirt.

I used to lead the line for Red Bull Salzburg and Dortmund.

I helped my club win the UEFA Champions League in 2023.

I scored 50 English top-flight goals in my first 48 matches – a new record.

THE MYSTERY PLAYER IS:

_____

34

SAFE HANDS

**This crossword is full of the best goalkeepers in the game.
Can you answer the clues and complete the grid?**

DOWN

1. Brazilian _____ Becker marshals the Liverpool goal line (7)
2. Mary _____ represents Manchester United and England (5)
4. Former Chelsea 'keeper ____ Čech holds the record for most English top-flight clean sheets (4)
5. Everton No. 1 Jordan _____ is an England hero (8)
7. Englishman ___ Foster has conceded more English top-flight goals than any other keeper (3)

ACROSS

3. A true pro, veteran _____ Neuer has played for Bayern Munich and Germany for years (6)
6. Brilliant Belgian Thibaut _____ is at home at the Bernabéu (8)
7. With 176 appearances for Italy, keeper Gianluigi _____ is a record breaker (6)

VAR REPLAY

The ref needs your help again on a key decision,
as only two of these instant replay images match
exactly. Can you work out which two are the same?

DIFFICULTY:

_____ and _____ are the same.

36 Answer on page 85.

DIFFICULTY:

AT MAXIMUM CAPACITY

These stadiums are famous for hosting epic action with huge crowds! But some of these stats aren't correct. Can you circle the four incorrect capacities?

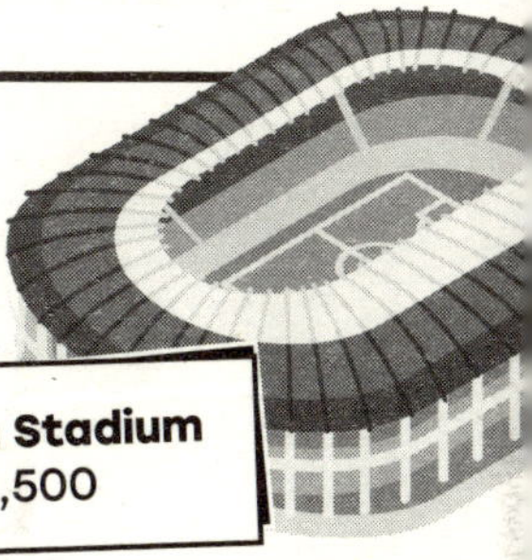

Old Trafford
45,009

London Stadium
62,500

Tottenham Hotspur Stadium
62,850

AmEx Stadium
71,928

Stamford Bridge
19,265

Selhurst Park
25,486

Etihad Stadium
53,400

Craven Cottage
54,001

Answers on page 85.

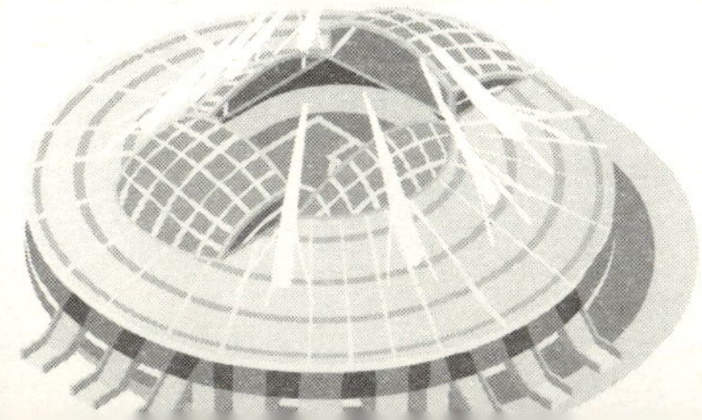

FOOTY FORMATIONS

**Add the missing pictures in these grids so each
column, row and box contains only one of each symbol.**

NOVICE

KEY:

SEMI-PRO

KEY:

How quickly did you do the
first two? Give yourself a
challenge and time yourself
for the next one!

KEY:

PRO

WORLD CLASS

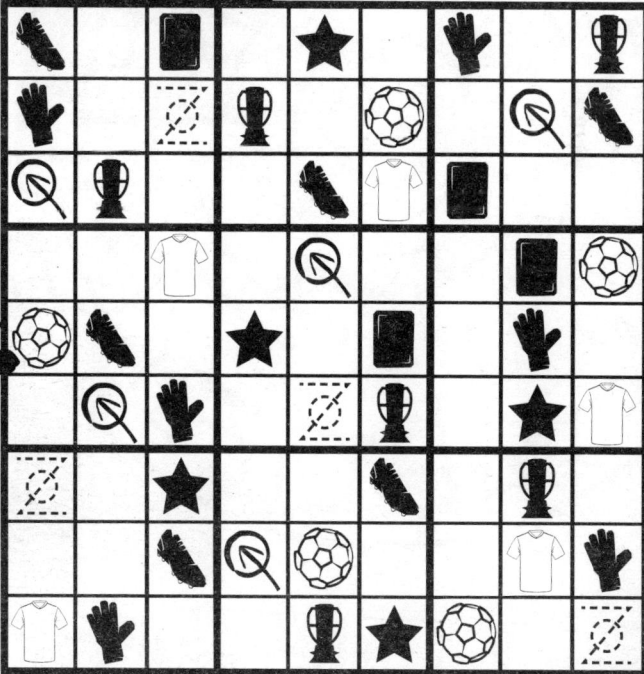

KEY:

BALL BONANZA

Time how long it takes you to navigate through this maze
and count how many balls you pass on the way!

START

FINISH

I did it in _ _ _ _ _ _ _ _ seconds

and collected _ _ _ _ _ _ _ balls!

ODD CLUB OUT

One of these teams doesn't belong in this list of European champions. Circle the odd club out!

Manchester City

Barcelona

Chelsea

Southampton

Inter Milan

Real Madrid

Bayern Munich

Liverpool

AC Milan

Answer on page 86.

BRILLIANT BELLINGHAM

In his first season at Real Madrid, Jude Bellingham confirmed himself as one of the greatest players on the planet. Draw a line between these epic statements and their answers!

Test yourself! Set a timer for 1 minute. Can you match them all in time?

1 Jude left this club to sign for Spanish giants Real Madrid.

Iran

17

2 In 2020, Bellingham made his senior England debut at this age.

3 Jude scored this record-breaking number of goals in his first 15 matches for Real Madrid.

Sunderland

Birmingham

4 In the World Cup in 2022, Bellingham's first England goal came against this team.

5 Bellingham began his career in the youth academy for this club.

14

Borussia Dortmund

6 His younger brother Jobe plays for this club.

WINGER WORDSEARCH

Can you find all 10 superstar wingers in this wordsearch? Their names can be forwards, backwards, up, down or diagonal!

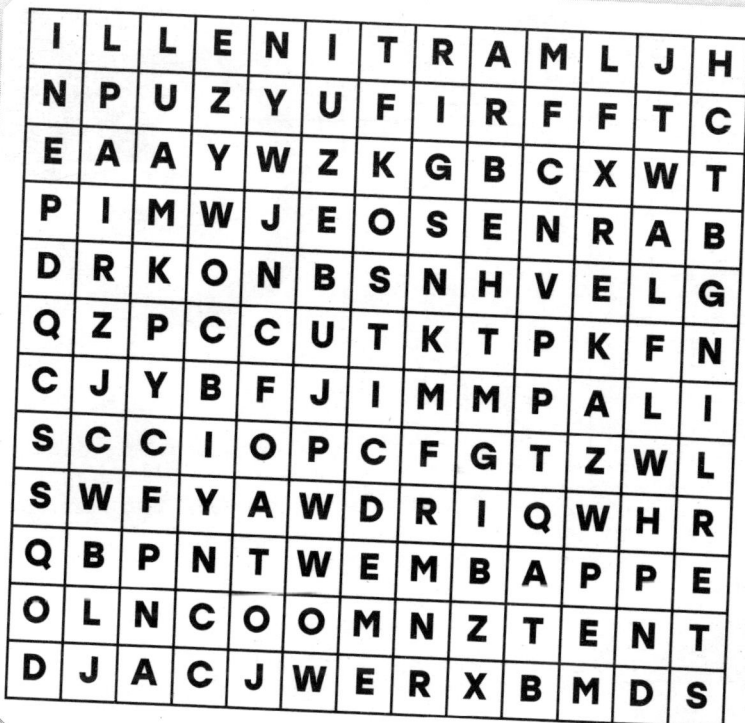

I	L	L	E	N	I	T	R	A	M	L	J	H
N	P	U	Z	Y	U	F	I	R	F	F	T	C
E	A	A	Y	W	Z	K	G	B	C	X	W	T
P	I	M	W	J	E	O	S	E	N	R	A	B
D	R	K	O	N	B	S	N	H	V	E	L	G
Q	Z	P	C	C	U	T	K	T	P	K	F	N
C	J	Y	B	F	J	I	M	M	P	A	L	I
S	C	C	I	O	P	C	F	G	T	Z	W	L
S	W	F	Y	A	W	D	R	I	Q	W	H	R
Q	B	P	N	T	W	E	M	B	A	P	P	E
O	L	N	C	O	O	M	N	Z	T	E	N	T
D	J	A	C	J	W	E	R	X	B	M	D	S

○ **BOWEN** ○ **COMAN** ○ **MARTINELLI**

○ **KOSTIĆ** ○ **JOTA** ○ **STERLING**

○ **FATI** ○ **DÍAZ**

○ **BARNES** ○ **MBAPPÉ**

PASS MASTER

**Can you pass your way out of each of these footy mazes?
Time how long it takes you to reach the end!**

START

I found my way out in

_____ minutes, _____ seconds.

FINISH

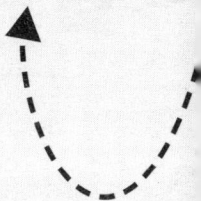

Answer on page 87.

DIFFICULTY:

SPANISH LEAGUE

The best teams in Spain play thrilling football with amazing skill and stamina. How well do you know the Spanish top-flight league?

1 Which team has won the Spanish top-flight league an amazing 35 times?

A. Real Madrid
B. Alavés
C. Sevilla
D. Real Sociedad

- - - - - - - - - - -

2 Barca hero Lionel Messi is the record goalscorer in the league's history. How many goals did he score in total?

A. 101   C. 99
B. 474   D. 321

- - - - - - - - - -

3 Two players have scored eight hat-tricks in a single season. Who were they?

A. Messi and Ronaldo
B. Messi and Griezmann
C. Messi and Bellingham
D. Messi and Lewandowski

- - - - - - - - - - - - - - - - - -

4 Which team plays all of its home matches at the Reale Arena?

A. Villareal
B. Barcelona
C. Real Madrid
D. Real Sociedad

- - - - - - - - - - - -

5 There are two teams from Madrid competing in the Spanish top flight. Can you name them?

A. Real Madrid and Atlético Madrid
B. Barcelona and Real Zaragoza
C. Alavés and Sevilla
D. Real Sociedad and Atlético Madrid

- -

6 Which club play its home matches in white and green striped jerseys?

A. Girona **C.** Valencia
B. Barcelona **D.** Real Betis

7 How many clubs compete in the Spanish top-flight league each season?

A. 14 **C.** 28
B. 20 **D.** 8

----

8 What name is given to the epic matches between Barcelona and Real Madrid?

A. Money Cup **C.** El Clásico
B. Tapas Trophy **D.** El Big Match

9 Barcelona forward Lamine Yamal is the youngest goalscorer in Spanish top-flight history. How old was he?

A. 12 **C.** 15
B. 21 **D.** 16

----

10 Which club has finished second place the most number of times in the Spanish top flight?

A. Real Betis
B. Barcelona
C. Valencia
D. Real Madrid

Answers on page 88.

MYSTERY PLAYER 3

**These statements are only true of one player,
but do you know who they describe?**

I've played for Atlético Madrid and Barcelona.

In 2018, I scored loads as I helped France win the World Cup.

I play anywhere across the forward line and can finish with both feet.

One of my goal celebrations was a Fortnite emote!

THE MYSTERY PLAYER IS:

_____

Answer on page 88.

DIFFICULTY: ⚽ ⚽

EURO DREAM TEAM

Wow, what an amazing starting lineup, but some of the names are incomplete. Can you fill them in before kick off?

E _ E _ S _ N
GK

CA _ _ E L _   S _ O N E _   SH _ W
RB   CB   LB

B _ R E L L _   _ I M _ I C H
CM   CM

B _ W E _   _ Í A Z
RW   LW

_ A N _   HA _ L _ N D   MBAP _ _
RF   CF   LF

EURO DREAM TEAM MANAGER'S NAME

....

ODD PLAYER OUT

**One of these players doesn't belong in this list
of league winners. Circle the odd player out!**

Erling Haaland

Declan Rice

Raheem Sterling

Bernado Silva

Kyle Walker

Mohamed Salah

Virgil van Dijk

Jack Grealish

Alisson Becker

Answer on page 88.

ON THE LINE

These footy jokes are hilarious, but your opponent has removed the punchlines! Can you complete the jokes?

1. Which team loves ice cream? (.......)

2. What tea do footballers drink? (.......)

3. What is a goalkeeper's favourite dinner? (.......)

4. How did the pitch end up as a triangle? (.......)

5. Why aren't stadiums built in outer space? (.......)

6. How do players keep cool during a match? (.......)

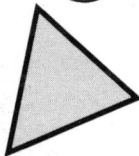

7. What is a ghost's favourite position? (.......)

8. What did the manager do when the pitch flooded? (.......)

A Somebody took a corner!

B They stand near the fans!

C Sent on some subs!

D Aston Vanilla!

E Penal-tea!

F Because there's no atmosphere!

G Ghoulkeeper!

H Beans on Post!

HEAD TO TOE

**This all-action footballer has been muddled up.
Can you put them back together in the correct order?**

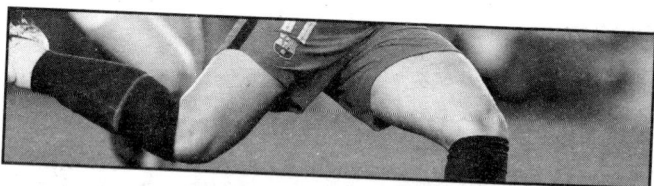

1

2

3

4

5

CORRECT ORDER:

____ ____ ____ ____ ____

BONUS!

WHO IS IT?

- -

ACROSS THE CITY

Manchester City are a dominant force in football. Can you cross the grid below following only the letters (in order) of MANCHESTER?

START →	M	A	M	A	N	C	H
C	A	C	R	E	T	R	E
C	N	C	H	M	S	S	S
M	N	E	E	M	E	M	T
R	E	T	S	M	H	H	E
M	A	E	A	N	C	M	R
E	N	M	M	H	C	A	C
H	C	H	R	R	C	N	H
E	S	T	E	E	H	A	N
S	H	C	H	S	C	S	E
A	M	R	E	T	S	R	FINISH →
N	C	H	E	S	T	E	M

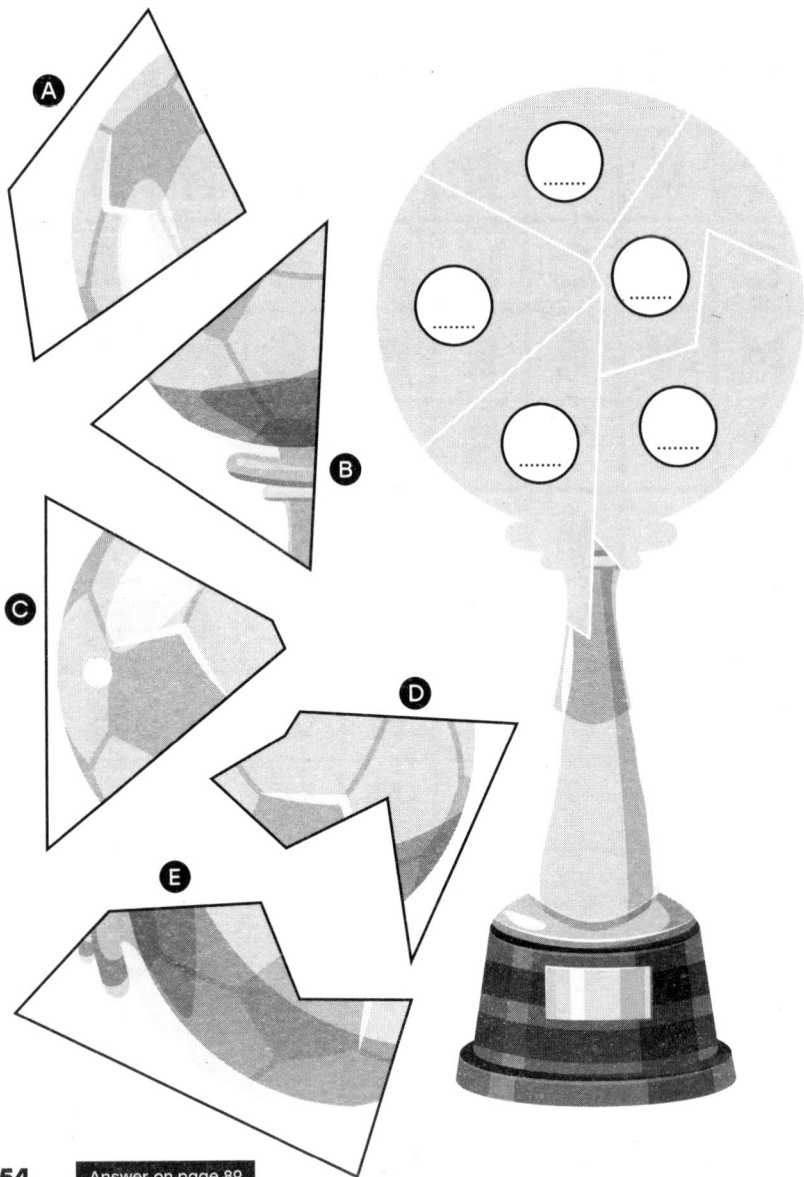

BROKEN BALL

**Whoa, this football-shaped trophy has been broken.
Can you work out how to reassemble it correctly?**

A

B

C

D

E

Answer on page 89.

PATTERN OF PLAY

Every team follows their own unique pattern of play. Complete the
sequences below by drawing the one missing image from each column.

TROPHY TROUBLE

Every player dreams of lifting a trophy, but one of these is a fake!
Which trophy is different to the others?

1

2

3

4

THE FAKE TROPHY IS:

Answer on page 89.

GOLDEN GOALS

These players have all achieved the ultimate goal - being top scorers in their leagues. Can you find them all in this grid?

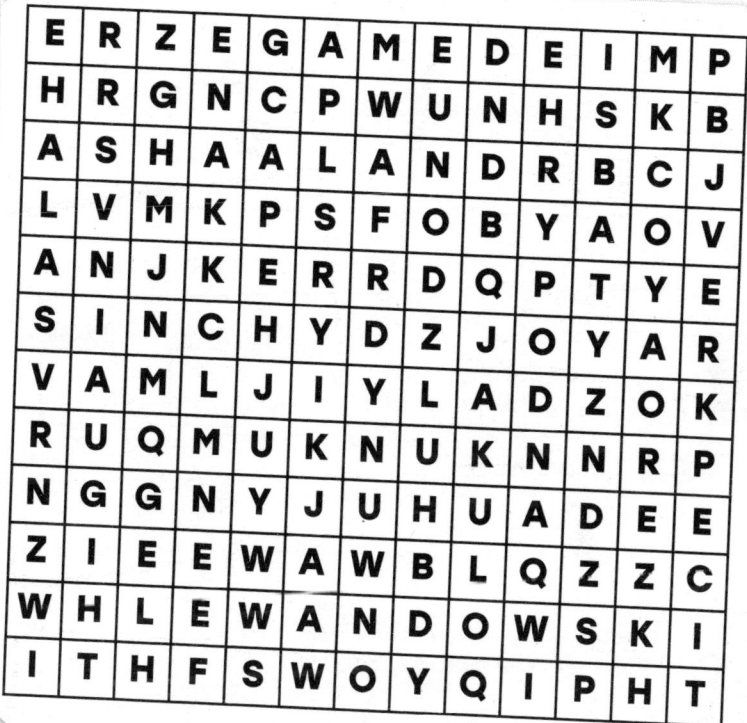

E	R	Z	E	G	A	M	E	D	E	I	M	P
H	R	G	N	C	P	W	U	N	H	S	K	B
A	S	H	A	A	L	A	N	D	R	B	C	J
L	V	M	K	P	S	F	O	B	Y	A	O	V
A	N	J	K	E	R	R	D	Q	P	T	Y	E
S	I	N	C	H	Y	D	Z	J	O	Y	A	R
V	A	M	L	J	I	Y	L	A	D	Z	O	K
R	U	Q	M	U	K	N	U	K	N	N	R	P
N	G	G	N	Y	J	U	H	U	A	D	E	E
Z	I	E	E	W	A	W	B	L	Q	Z	Z	C
W	H	L	E	W	A	N	D	O	W	S	K	I
I	T	H	F	S	W	O	Y	Q	I	P	H	T

- LEWANDOWSKI
- RONALDO
- SALAH
- NKUNKU
- KERR
- MIEDEMA
- DALY
- KANE
- HIGUAÍN
- HAALAND

I found them all in _____ minutes, _____ seconds.

FOOTY TRUE OR FALSE?

**These facts are out of this world – but some of them aren't true!
Put a tick on True or a cross on False on each one!**

1 England play their home matches at Wembley Stadium.

TRUE ☐ FALSE ☐

2 A football pitch has two centre spots.

TRUE ☐ FALSE ☐

3 Every team plays a match on Christmas day.

TRUE ☐ FALSE ☐

4 Italian club Juventus have never lost a match.

TRUE ☐ FALSE ☐

5 Leicester City play their home matches at the Bluepaw Arena.

TRUE ☐ FALSE ☐

6 England's crest is made up of three lions.

TRUE ☐ FALSE ☐

7 Kylian Mbappé is Paris Saint-Germain's record goalscorer in all competitions.

TRUE ☐ FALSE ☐

8 Scottish giants Celtic play in the English top-flight league

TRUE ☐ FALSE ☐

9 Top-flight referees must be able to sprint 100 metres in under 10 seconds.

TRUE ☐ FALSE ☐

10 Football matches are abandoned if it starts to snow.

TRUE ☐ FALSE ☐

Answers on page 90.

TRAINING PITCH

Training is over and the last one to the changing rooms has to tidy the pitch! Race through this maze as fast as you can!

START

FINISH

I did it in _ _ _ _ _ _ _ _ _ _ _ seconds.

ODD WORD OUT

One of these words isn't part of a football pitch, but which is it?

Centre circle

Goal line

Touch line

Half-way line

Corner arc

Penalty spot

VAR

Goal area

Penalty area

Answer on page 91.

MATCH ATTAX MIX-UP

**Another Match Attax card has been divided into five strips.
Your task is to put the card back together.
Can you work out what order the strips need to go in?**

1  **2**  **3**  **4**  **5**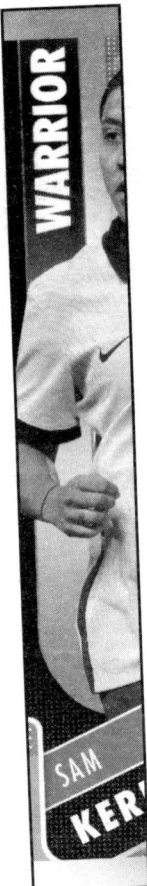

CORRECT ORDER:

___ ___ ___ ___ ___

MYSTERY PLAYER 4

**All these clues describe an Arsenal women's superstar!
Can you work out who it is?**

I've played for the Netherlands women's team over 117 times!

I'm a super striker but I love assisting my teammates too!

Since 2017, I've been scoring goals for fun for Arsenal women's team!

I was the first player to score 50 goals in the English women's top-flight league!

THE MYSTERY PLAYER IS:

MEMORY MADNESS

Read all the facts on these pages and try your best to memorise them, then turn the page and see how many you can remember!

HUGE STADIUM

Manchester United's Old Trafford is the biggest stadium in the English top-flight league, with a capacity of 74,310.

GERMAN GIANTS

Bayern Munich have lifted the UEFA Champions League trophy a mega-impressive six times!

LEGENDARY JUDE

Jude Bellingham scored 10 goals in his first 10 matches after his blockbuster transfer to Real Madrid.

MAGNIFICENT MILAN

Inter Milan have won the Italian top-flight league an incredible 19 times!

JACK'S MIDDLE NAME

Manchester City and England star Jack Grealish's middle name is Peter.

GOOD POINT

The most points ever scored in a season of the English top-flight league was 100 by Manchester City.

PORTUGAL POWER

The biggest stadium in the Portugese top-flight league is Benfica's Estádio da Luz, with 64,642 seats.

TOP SCORER

Lionel Messi is the top scorer across Europe's top leagues, with 496 career goals.

JACK'S MIDDLE NAME

What is Manchester City and England star Jack Grealish's middle name?

TOP SCORER

How many goals has Lionel Messi scored in European competition?

LEGENDARY JUDE

How many goals did Jude Bellingham score in his first 10 matches for Real Madrid?

GERMAN GIANTS

How many times have Bayern Munich won the UEFA Champions League?

PORTUGAL POWER

How many seats does Benfica's Estádio da Luz stadium contain?

MAGNIFICENT MILAN

How many times have Inter Milan won the Italian top-flight league?

HUGE STADIUM

What is the capacity of Manchester United's stadium, Old Trafford?

GOOD POINT

Only one team has ever reached 100 points in an English top-flight league season. Who was it?

FOOTY FORMATIONS

It's time for more sudoku fun! Draw the missing pictures in these grids
so each column, row and box contains only one of each symbol.

NOVICE

KEY:

SEMI-PRO

KEY:

KEY:

PRO

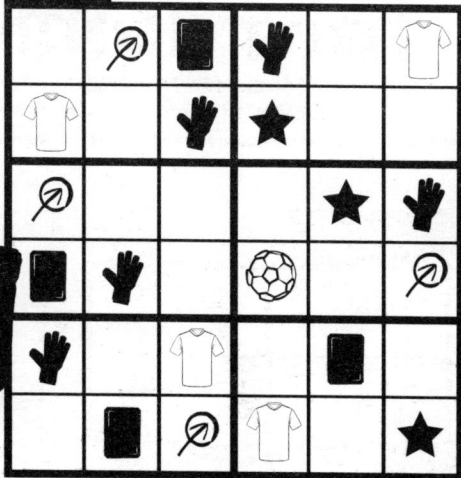

WORLD CLASS

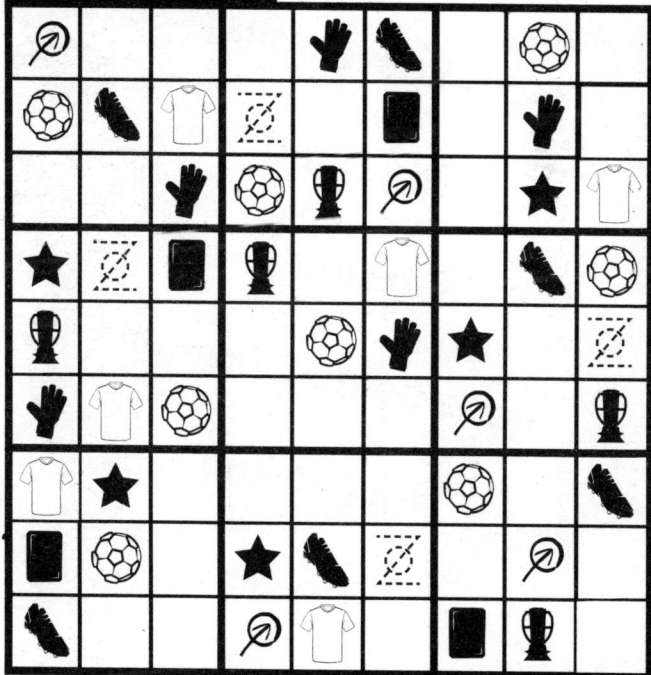

KEY:

DIFFICULTY:

TOP-FLIGHT LEAGUE

One of these teams doesn't play in the top-flight league in their country, but which is it?

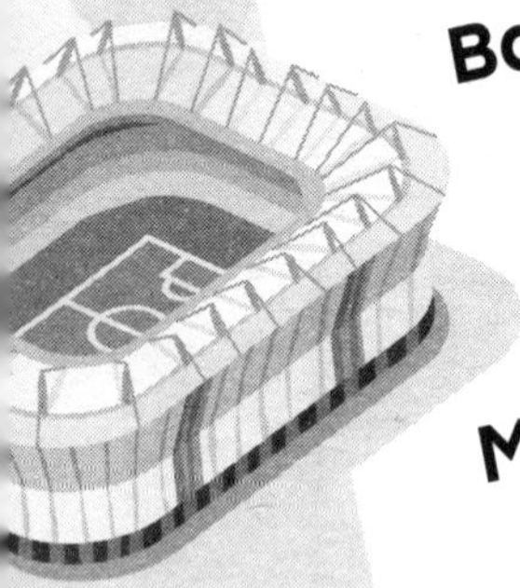

Real Zaragoza

Bayern Munich

Real Madrid

Manchester City

Barcelona

Arsenal

Paris Saint-Germain

Inter Milan

Celtic

Answer on page 94.

MYSTERY PLAYER 5

Can you read the clues and identify which mystery player is being described?

In international matches, I play for the team known as Les Bleus.

I am one of only two players to ever score a hat-trick in a World Cup final.

In the 2020-21 French top-flight season, I finished top scorer and top assister!

I am famous for my dribbling skills and explosive acceleration.

THE MYSTERY PLAYER IS:

_____

Answer on page 94.

MANAGER OR REFEREE?

Each of these names is famous but do they belong to a manager or referee? Write your answers underneath!

1. Michael Oliver

----

2. David Moyes

----

3. Mikel Arteta

----

4. Craig Pawson

----

5. Gary O'Neil

----

6. Stuart Attwell

----

7. Jürgen Klopp

----

8. Pep Guardiola

THE MADRID DERBY

Real Madrid and Atlético Madrid love a good derby! Can you make your way across this grid following only the letters (in order) of MADRID?

START →	M	A	M	A	D	R	M
M	E	D	R	E	E	D	I
A	I	I	I	D	T	S	R
M	A	M	I	M	E	M	I
R	I	R	D	A	D	I	D
M	A	I	M	D	M	A	M
I	R	D	M	A	D	A	I
D	M	I	D	I	R	D	D
M	R	I	M	M	M	A	M
I	D	R	A	D	M	I	D
D	M	R	M	R	I	D	FINISH →
D	I	R	D	M	R	I	M

SUPER WOMEN

This crossword is all about the best players in the women's top-flight league! Can you answer the clues and complete the grid?

DOWN

1. Sam ____ is a goal machine for Chelsea (4)
3. Sophie _____ is the record appearance holder in the women's top-flight league (5)
5. Bethany England plays for _____ Hotspur (9)
6. Aged 16 years, Lauren ____ is the youngest ever goalscorer in the league! (4)
7. _____ Women won the league title every season from 2019 to 2023 (7)

ACROSS

2. The biggest attendance was 60,160 at Arsenal's _____ Stadium (8)
4. Vivianne _____ once scored 22 goals in one season (7)
8. Bescot Stadium is the home of _____ Villa Women (5)

GOAL OR DEFENCE?

Each of these players is famous for thrilling fans around Europe, but what are they famous for – defending or playing in goal?

1. Nayef Aguerd

----

2. Ederson

----

3. Virgil van Dijk

----

4. John Stones

----

5. Alisson

----

6. Alphonse Areola

----

7. Lewis Dunk

----

8. Jordan Pickford

Answer on page 95.

75

ANSWERS

PAGE 6

CORRECT ORDER: 2, 4, 3, 5, 1

JUDE BELLINGHAM

MID

10.5M

Topps

DEFENCE
85

ATTACK
93

— EMERALD LIMITED EDITION —

PAGE 7

1 True	**6** True
2 False	**7** False
3 True	**8** False
4 True	**9** False
5 False	**10** True

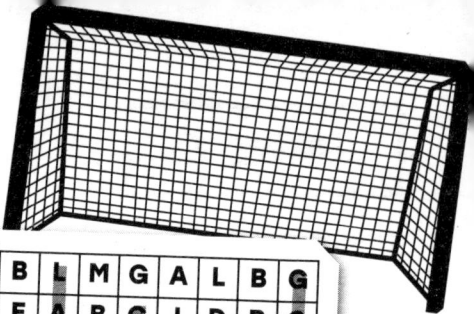

G	D	A	O	S	B	L	M	G	A	L	B	G
B	O	G	A	O	E	A	B	G	I	D	R	O
M	L	A	D	I	M	O	U	O	O	S	M	A
O	D	U	L	A	O	G	A	A	E	A	G	L
O	A	R	M	G	R	D	B	L	M	B	L	A
G	O	A	L	U	G	L	A	I	D	L	U	S
S	B	G	E	B	E	G	S	G	R	O	A	A
L	D	U	I	L	L	O	E	L	A	O	G	B
A	M	G	R	O	D	A	M	A	B	A	D	M
O	B	O	A	M	B	L	O	O	L	G	D	O
G	A	A	U	S	A	G	E	G	E	A	E	B
B	S	L	E	D	E	I	M	D	O	I	O	S
G	O	G	O	A	L	B	L	R	A	U	B	G

15 GOALS!

THEIR LEFT BACK
IS TIRED.
ATTACK THEM!

PAGE 10

2 and **3** are the same.

PAGE 11

1 213	**4** 8
2 18	**5** 46
3 10, 18, 37	**6** 0

PAGE 12

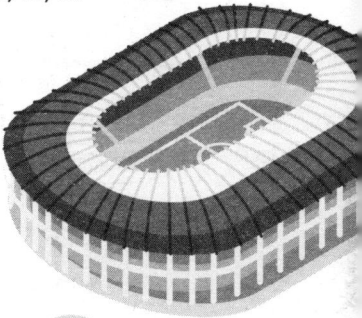

(A)
(B)
(C)

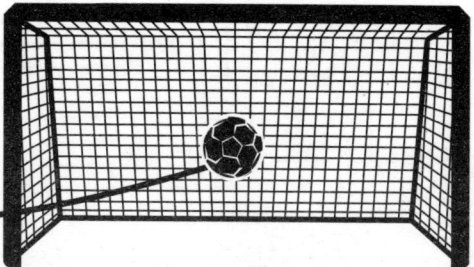

PAGE 13

SPAIN BARCELONA
FRANCE PARIS SAINT-GERMAIN
GERMANY BAYERN MUNICH

ENGLAND MANCHESTER CITY
ITALY INTER MILAN
SCOTLAND CELTIC

PAGE 14

PAGE 15

1 RASHFORD
2 MADDISON
3 HAALAND
4 KUDUS
5 MESSI

PAGES 16-17

1 A. 91
2 C. Borussia Dortmund
3 B. RB Leipzig
4 B. 41
5 A. 7 (most recently, Erling Haaland for Borussia Dortmund)
6 D. Werder Bremen
7 D. 2022-23 (Bayern Munich were champions on goal difference)
8 B. Thomas Müller
9 A. Gerd Müller
10 B. Cheeseburger XL

PAGE 18

Borussia Dortmund - BVB Stadion
Paris Saint-Germain - Parc des Princes
Manchester United - Old Trafford
SSC Napoli - Stadio Diego Armando Maradona
Arsenal - Emirates Stadium
Real Madrid - Santiago Bernabéu Stadium

PAGE 19

1 Attack	5 Defend
2 Attack	6 Attack
3 Defend	7 Attack
4 Attack	8 Defend

PAGES 20-21

1 Alisson	7 Son
11 Watkins	17 De Bruyne
20 Bowen	41 Rice
8 Fernandes	23 Gallagher

PAGE 22

There are **30** balls.

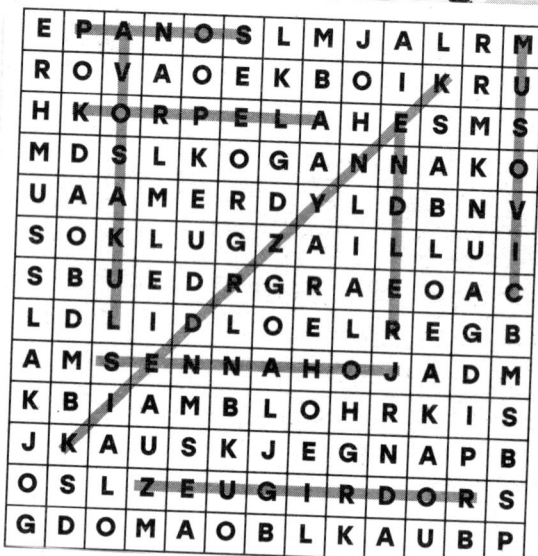

E	P	A	N	O	S	L	M	J	A	L	R	M
R	O	V	A	O	E	K	B	O	I	K	R	U
H	K	O	R	P	E	L	A	H	E	S	M	S
M	D	S	L	K	O	G	A	N	N	A	K	O
U	A	A	M	E	R	D	Y	L	D	B	N	V
S	O	K	L	U	G	Z	A	I	L	L	U	I
S	B	U	E	D	R	G	R	A	E	O	A	C
L	D	L	I	D	L	O	E	L	R	E	G	B
A	M	S	E	N	N	A	H	O	J	A	D	M
K	B	I	A	M	B	L	O	H	R	K	I	S
J	K	A	U	S	K	J	E	G	N	A	P	B
O	S	L	Z	E	U	G	I	R	D	O	R	S
G	D	O	M	A	O	B	L	K	A	U	B	P

PAGES 24-25

1 D. Manchester City
2 C. 1
3 A. Goalkeeper
4 A. David Beckham
5 A. 123

6 C. 6
7 D. Southampton
8 C. Liverpool
9 B. Aston Villa
10 B. Old Trafford

PAGE 26

PLAYER 1: İlkay Gündoğan
PLAYER 2: Virgil van Dijk
PLAYER 3: Jude Bellingham
PLAYER 4: Sergi Roberto

PAGE 27

CORRECT ORDER: 5, 3, 1, 4, 2

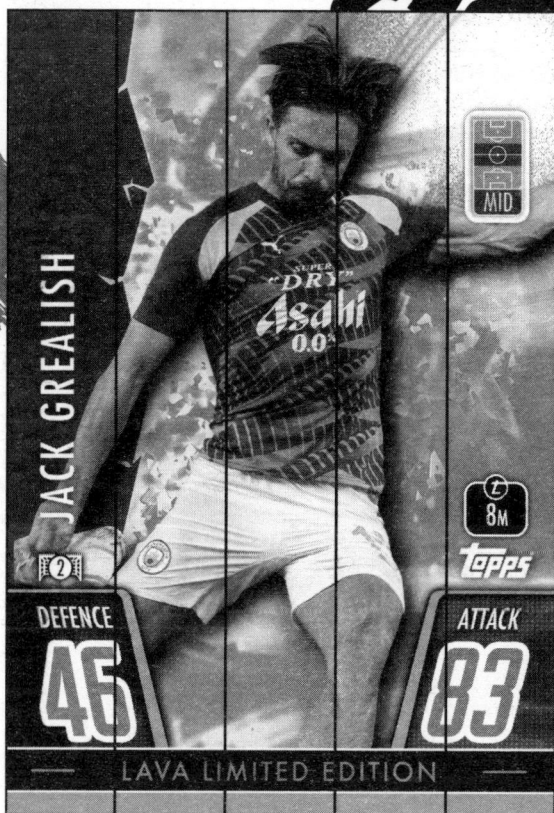

JACK GREALISH

MID

8M

Topps

DEFENCE
46

ATTACK
83

LAVA LIMITED EDITION

PAGE 28

1 BRAZIL
2 ENGLAND
3 ARGENTINA
4 SPAIN

5 MEXICO
6 URUGUAY
7 JAPAN
8 FRANCE

PAGE 29

The mystery player is
Declan Rice.

West Ham UEFA Europa Conference League
Manchester City UEFA Champions League
Sevilla UEFA Europa League
Barcelona Spanish Champions
Paris Saint-Germain French Champions
Napoli Italian Champions
Bayern Munich German Champions
Celtic Scottish Champions

PAGES 32-33

1. A.12
2. D. Chelsea
3. C. Rachel Daly (Aston Villa)
4. B. 2nd (2022-23)
5. A. Vivianne Miedema
6. D. 33
7. A. 60,160
8. B. 16
9. D. Chelsea
10. B. Two hat-tricks

PAGE 34

The mystery player is **Erling Haaland.**

PAGE 35

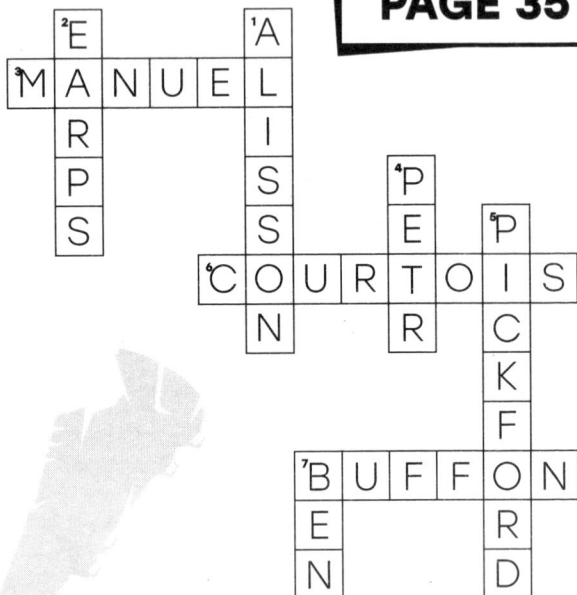

PAGE 36

1 and **5** are the same.

PAGE 37

These stadiums were false:

Old Trafford:
should be 74,310
AmEx Stadium:
should be 31,876
Stamford Bridge:
should be 40,341
Craven Cottage:
should be 25,700

PAGES 38-39

NOVICE

SEMI-PRO

PRO

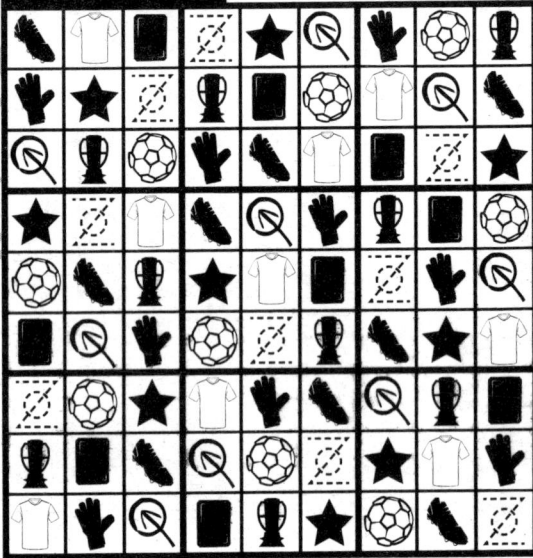

WORLD CLASS

PAGE 40

You should have collected **eight footballs**.

START

FINISH

PAGE 41

Southampton are the only club that haven't won the UEFA Champions League.

PAGE 42

PAGE 43

1 Borussia Dortmund
2 17
3 14
4 Iran
5 Birmingham
6 Sunderland

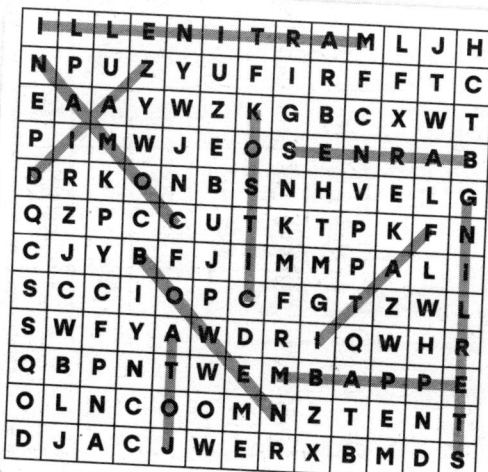

PAGES 44-45

PAGES 46-47

1 A. Real Madrid
2 B. 474
3 A. Lionel Messi and Cristiano Ronaldo
4 D. Real Sociedad
5 A. Real Madrid and Atlético Madrid
6 D. Real Betis
7 B. 20
8 C. El Clásico
9 D. 16
10 B. Barcelona

PAGE 48

The mystery player is **Antoine Griezmann**.

PAGE 49

GK Ederson
RB Cancelo
CB Stones
LB Shaw
CM Barella
CM Kimmich
RW Bowen
LW Díaz
RF Kane
CF Haaland
CF Mbappé

PAGE 50

Declan Rice is the only player who hasn't won the English top-flight league.

PAGE 51

1 D
2 E
3 H
4 A
5 F
6 B
7 G
8 C

PAGE 52

5
2
4
1
3

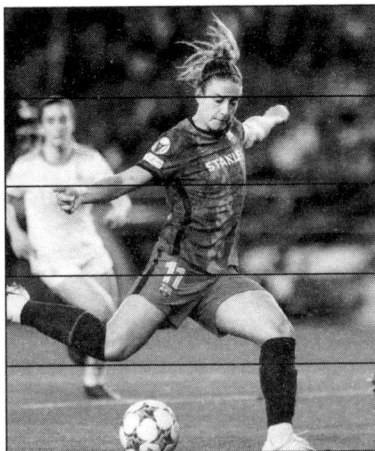

Bonus Question: **Alexia Putellas**.

PAGE 53

START	M	A	M	A	N	C	H
C	A	C	R	E	T	R	E
C	N	C	H	M	S	S	S
M	N	E	E	M	E	M	T
R	E	T	S	M	H	H	E
M	A	E	A	N	C	M	R
E	N	M	M	H	C	A	C
H	C	H	R	R	C	N	H
E	S	T	E	E	H	A	N
S	H	C	H	S	C	S	E
A	M	R	E	T	S	R	FINISH
N	C	H	E	S	T	E	M

PAGE 54

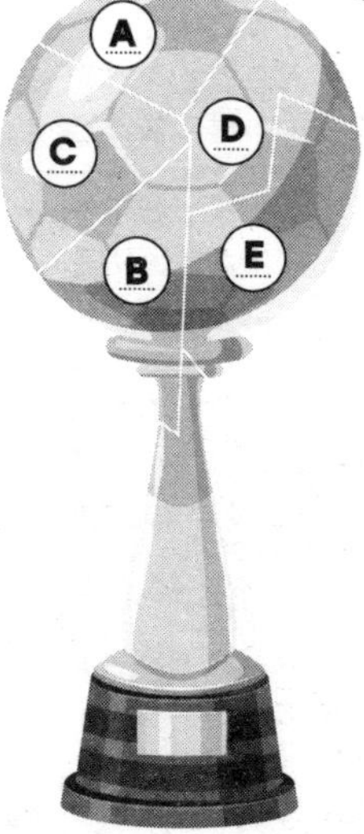

PAGE 55

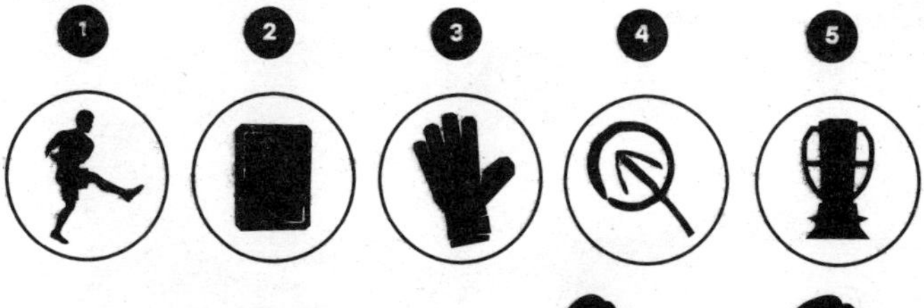

PAGE 56

The fake trophy is **3**.

E	R	Z	E	G	A	M	E	D	E	I	M	P
H	R	G	N	C	P	W	U	N	H	S	K	B
A	S	H	A	A	L	A	N	D	R	B	C	J
L	V	M	K	P	S	F	O	B	Y	A	O	V
A	N	J	K	E	R	R	D	Q	P	T	Y	E
S	I	N	C	H	Y	D	Z	J	O	Y	A	R
V	A	M	L	J	I	Y	L	A	D	Z	O	K
R	U	Q	M	U	K	N	U	K	N	N	R	P
N	G	G	N	Y	J	U	H	U	A	D	E	E
Z	I	E	E	W	A	W	B	L	Q	Z	Z	C
W	H	L	E	W	A	N	D	O	W	S	K	I
I	T	H	F	S	W	O	Y	Q	I	P	H	T

1 True
2 False
3 False
4 False
5 False
6 True
7 True
8 False
9 False
10 False

START

FINISH

PAGE 61

VAR isn't part of a football pitch.

PAGE 62

CORRECT ORDER: 2, 5, 3, 1, 4

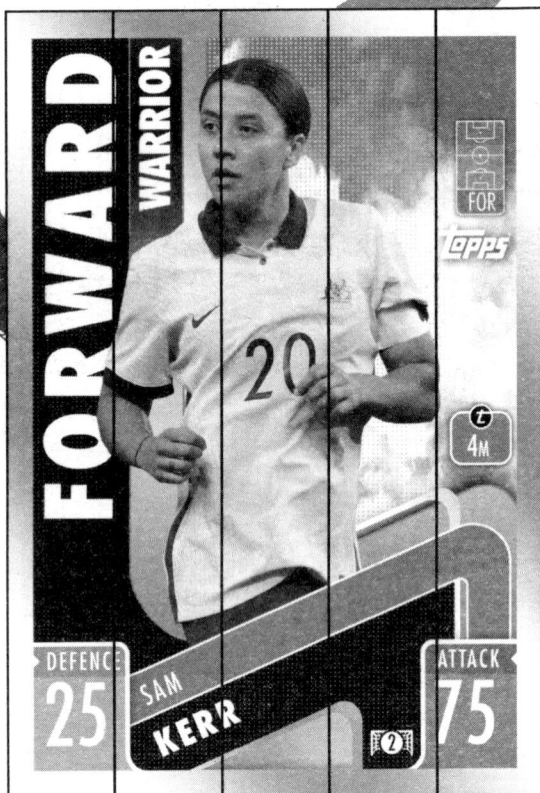

FORWARD

WARRIOR

FOR

Topps

4M

DEFENCE
25

SAM
KER'R

ATTACK
75

PAGE 63

The mystery player is
Vivianne Miedema.

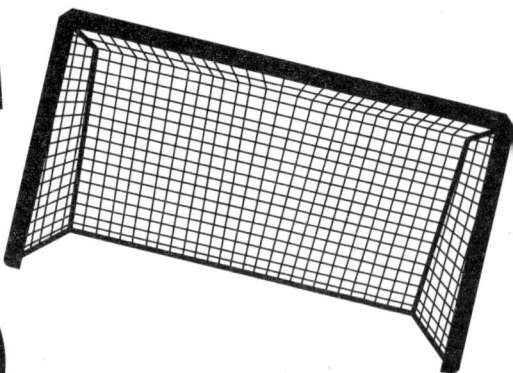

PAGES 64-67

Jack's Middle Name Peter
Top Scorer 496
Legendary Jude 10
German Giants Six

Portugal Power 64,642
Magnificent Milan 19
Huge Stadium 74,310
Good Point Manchester City

PAGES 68-69

NOVICE

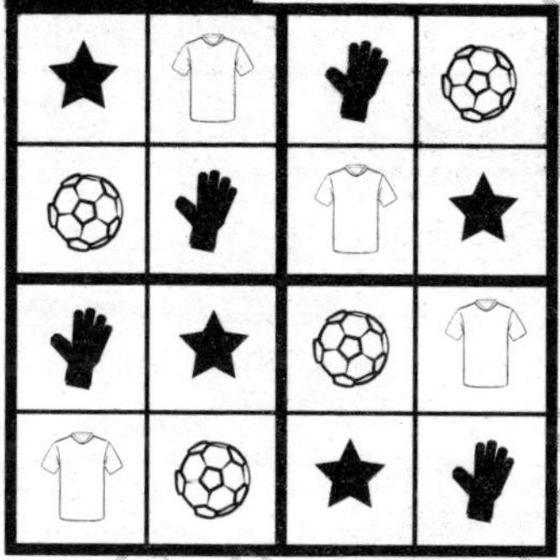

SEMI-PRO

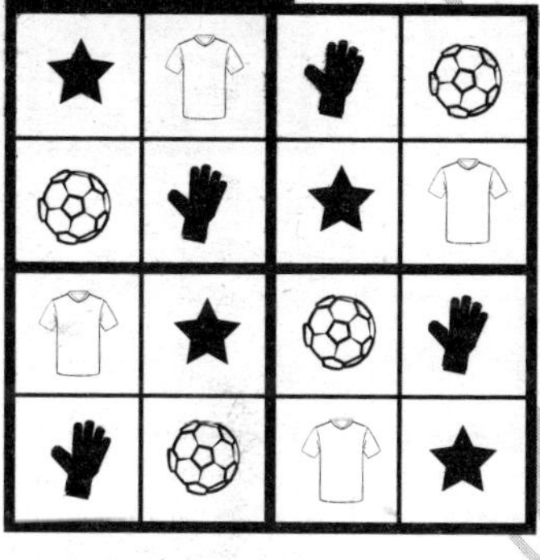

PRO

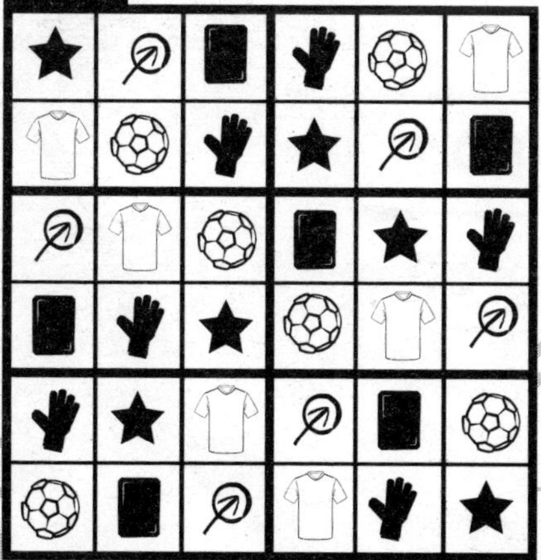

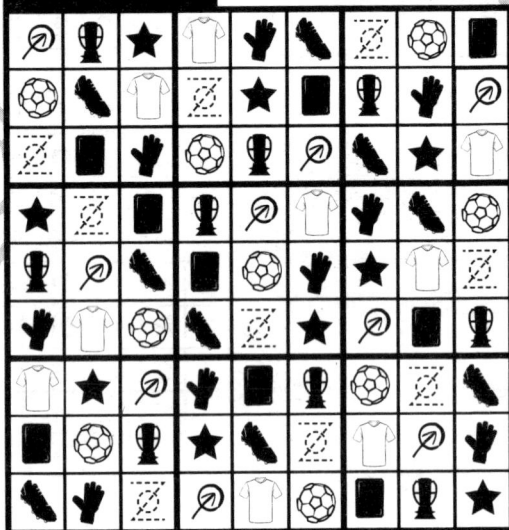

WORLD CLASS

PAGE 70

Real Zaragoza are the only club that aren't playing in their country's top-flight league.

PAGE 71

The mystery player is **Kylian Mbappé.**

PAGE 72

1 Referee
2 Manager
3 Manager
4 Referee
5 Manager
6 Referee
7 Manager
8 Manager

PAGE 73

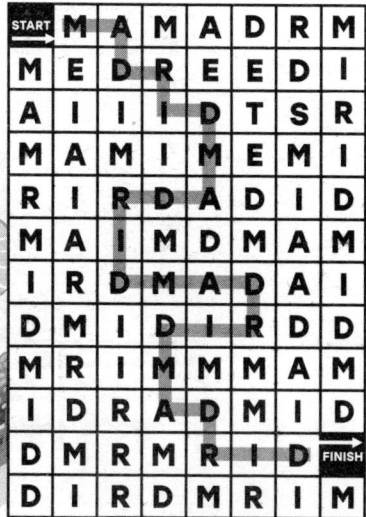

START	M	A	M	A	D	R	M
M	E	D	R	E	E	D	I
A	I	I	D	T	S	R
M	A	M	I	M	E	M	I
R	I	R	D	A	D	I	D
M	A	I	M	D	M	A	M
I	R	D	M	A	D	A	I
D	M	I	D	I	R	D	D
M	R	I	M	M	M	A	M
I	D	R	A	D	M	I	D
D	M	R	M	R	I	D	FINISH
D	I	R	D	M	R	I	M

PAGE 74

Crossword:

5. T O T T E N H A M (down)
7. C H E L S E E (down)
1. K E R R (down)
2. E M I R A T E S (across)
8. A S T O N (across)
3. I N G L E (down)
6. H E M P (down)
4. M I E D E M A (across)

PAGE 75

1 Defender
2 Goalkeeper
3 Defender
4 Defender
5 Goalkeeper
6 Goalkeeper
7 Defender
8 Goalkeeper

topps

MATCH
☆☆☆☆☆
ATTAX
®

TRADING CARD GAME

uk.topps.com